WONDERFULLY BAD

DAD JOKES

A MESSAGE TO DAD

____

____

____

____

FOLLOW US AT:

 @DADJOKES1

 @DADJOKES01

WWW.DADJOKESGIFT.COM

1, 3, 5, 7, AND 9 WANTED TO FIGHT ME.

I SAID NO BECAUSE THE ODDS WERE AGAINST ME.

THERE WAS AN EXPLOSION AT A FRENCH CHEESE SHOP.

DA BRIE EVERYWHERE.

WHY ARE GROUPS OF MOUNTAINS FUNNY?

BECAUSE THEY ARE HILL AREAS.

WHO CAN CARRY PETROL?

JERRY CAN.

WHAT DO YOU CALL A SAD ROBOT?

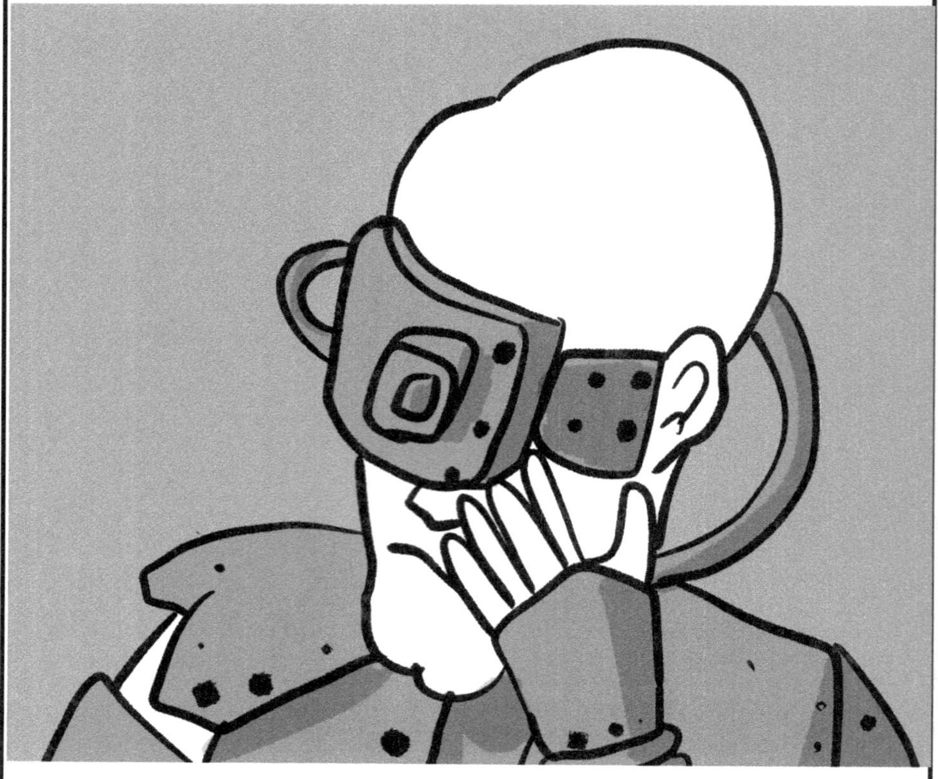

A SIGH BORG.

I SPENT $100 ON A BELT THAT DIDN'T FIT.

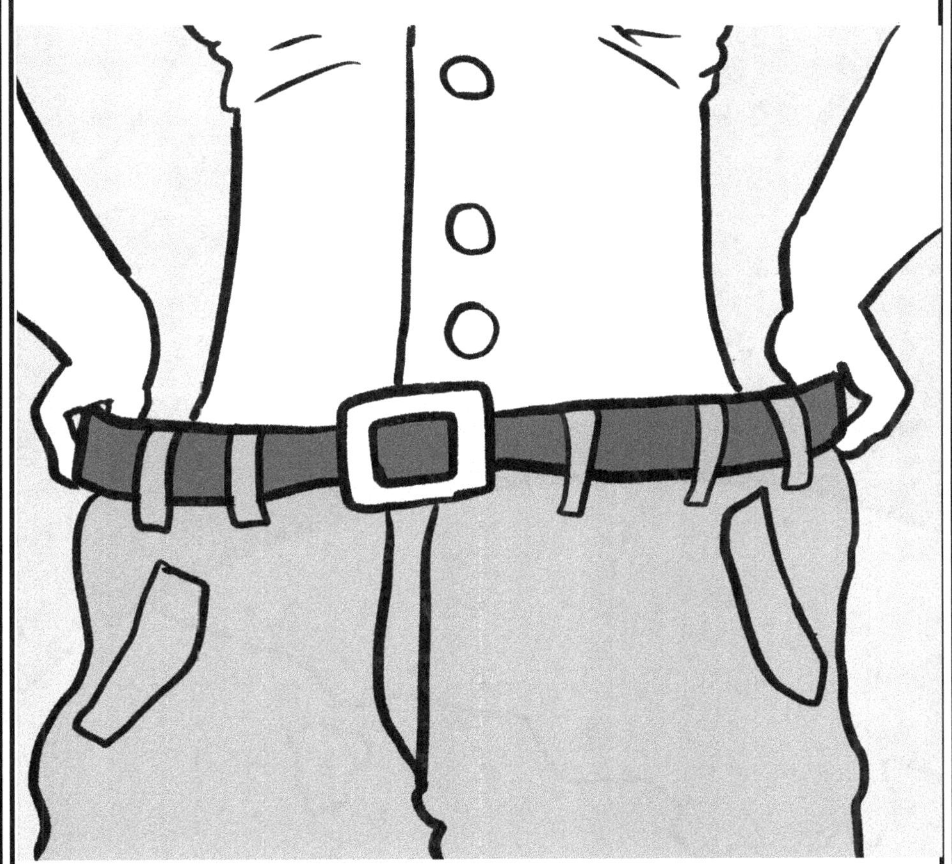

IT WAS A HUGE WAIST.

THE WAY THE EARTH ROTATES MAKES ME FEEL HAPPY.

IT REALLY MAKES MY DAY.

WHAT'S THE NAME FOR A FAT PSYCHIC?

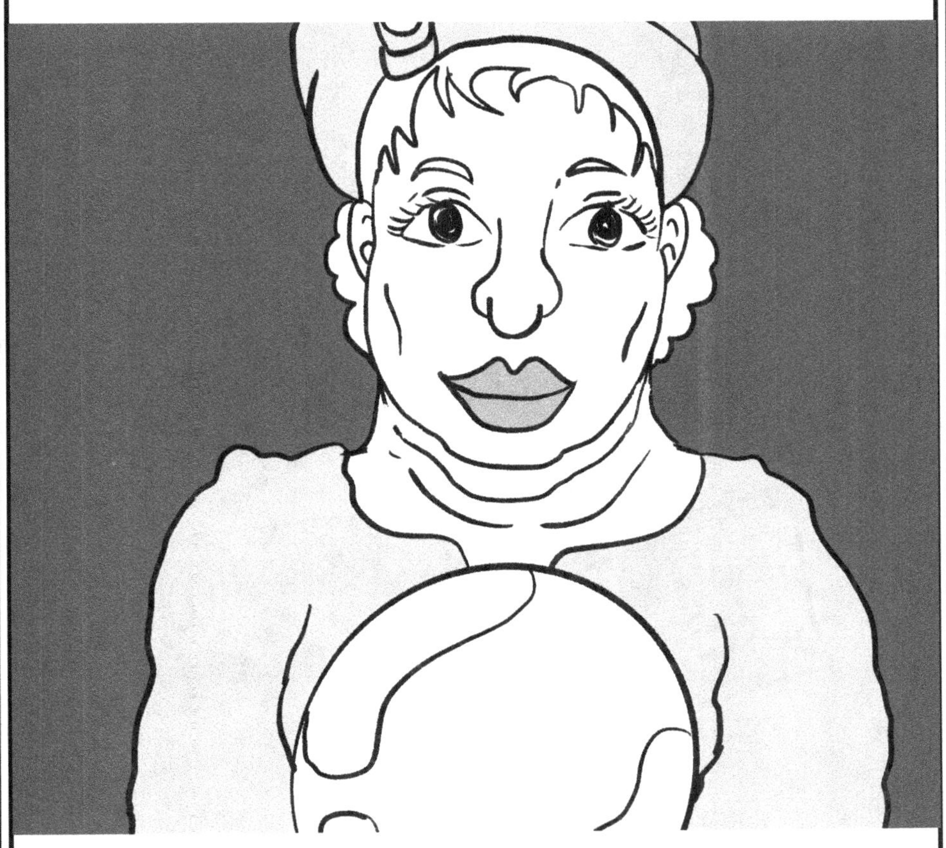

A FOUR CHIN TELLER.

YOU DON'T HAVE TO PAY FOR DEAD BATTERIES.

THEY ARE FREE OF CHARGE.

THERE WAS AN ARGUMENT ABOUT THE MOST IMPORTANT VOWEL.

I WON.

DO YOU KNOW HOW TO TELL THE DIFFERENCE BETWEEN A JEWELER AND A JAILER?

ONE SELLS WATCHES AND THE OTHER WATCHES CELLS.

I DON'T HAVE A DAD BODY.

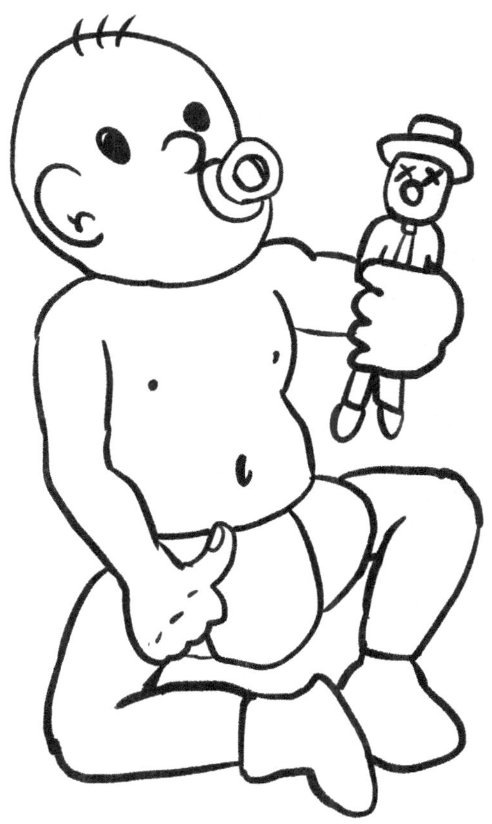

I HAVE A FATHER FIGURE.

WHAT DID THE HAIR SAY WHEN it WENT to THE BARBERS?

HAIR WE GO!

I WAS THINKING ABOUT THE last TIME I PUT MY CAR IN REVERSE.

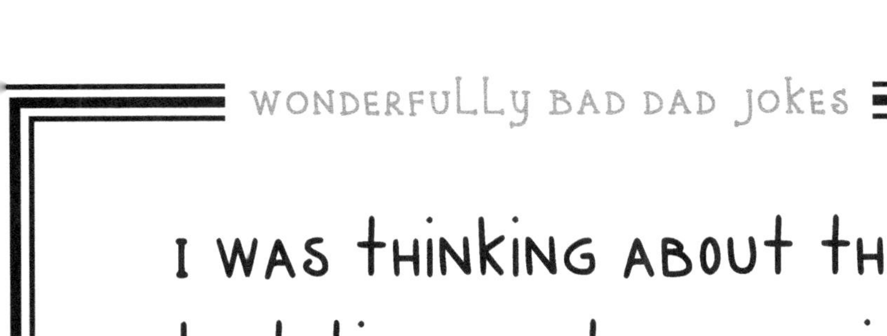

THAT TAKES ME BACK.

HOW DO YOU MAKE A DUCK A SINGER?

put it in the oven till it's Bill Withers.

SOMEONE STOLE MY GLASSES.

JOKE'S ON HIM AS I CAN STILL DRINK FROM THE BOTTLE.

TOO MANY PEOPLE ARE JUDGEMENTAL.

I CAN tell BY looking At THEM.

MY WIFE CALLS ME CHEAP.

BUT I'M NOT BUYING IT.

WHY ARE BULLETS BAD EMPLOYEES?

THEY ONLY WORK AFTER THEY'VE BEEN FIRED.

WHAT DID THE HAT tell THE SCARF?

YOU HANG AROUND HERE; I'll GO ON AHEAD.

WHAT DO YOU CALL A SHIRT WITH PICTURES OF CORN ON?

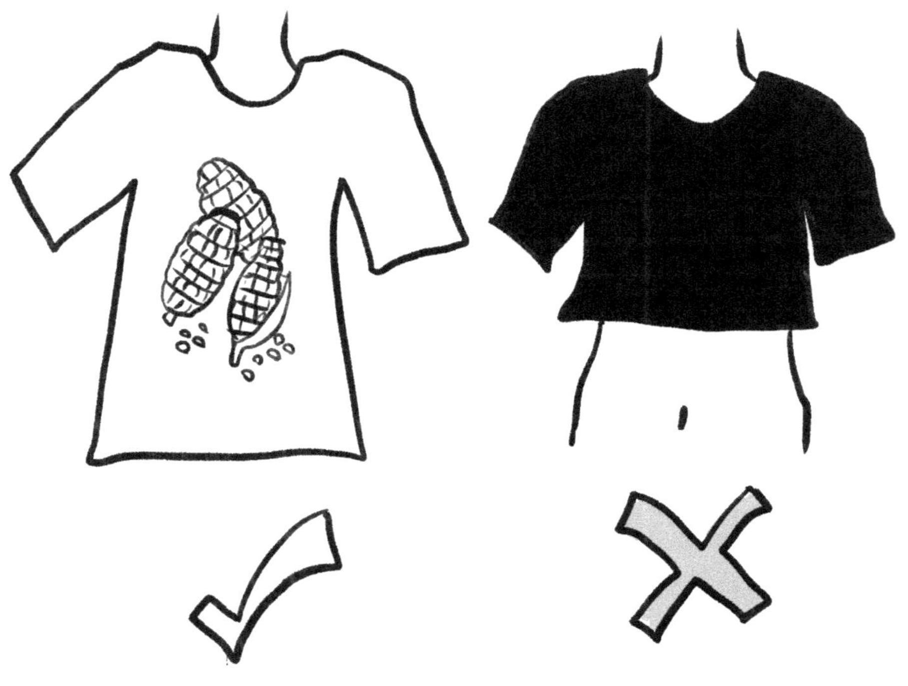

A CROP TOP.

HOW DO YOU QUIT BEING VEGAN?

COLD TURKEY.

THERE IS A POPULAR NEW BROOM.

IT'S SWEEPING THE NATION.

MY PERSONAL TRAINER KEEPS laughing WHEN HE tells ME to USE A treadmill.

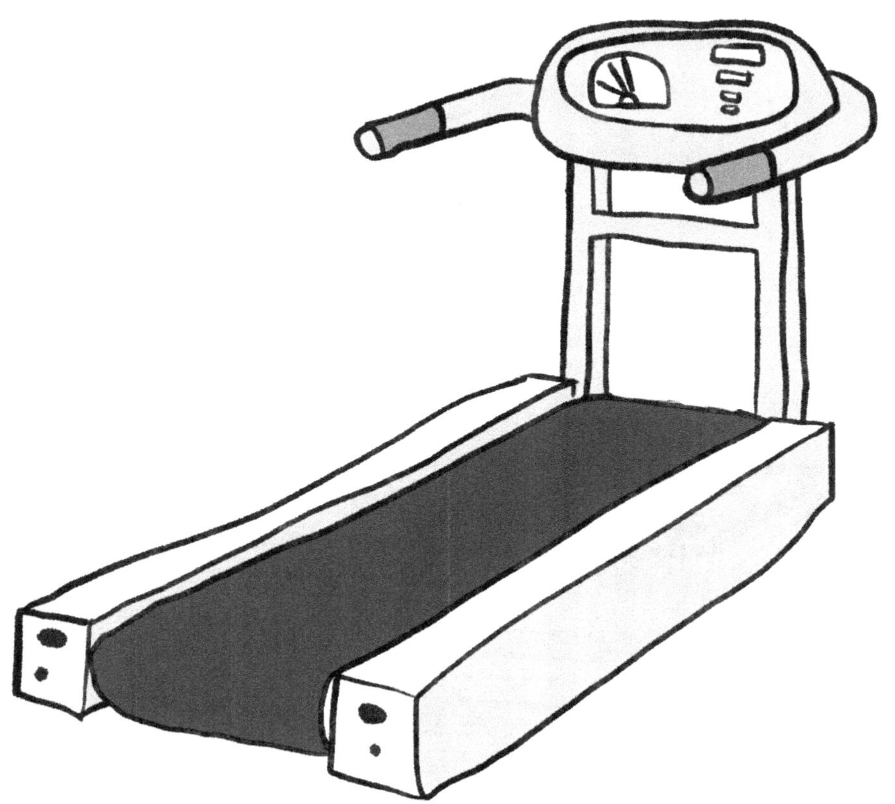

I GUESS it's A RUNNING joke.

WHEN CAN'T SAILORS PLAY CARDS?

WHENEVER SOMEONE IS STANDING ON THE DECK.

CEMETERIES ARE IN THE MIDDLE OF TOWNS

THE DEAD CENTRE.

SOME STORES DON'T ACCEPT SMALL COINS

THE POLICY MAKES NO CENTS.

HOW DO YOU GET A COMPUTER DRUNK?

WITH SCREEN SHOTS.

WHY DO FRENCH PEOPLE ONLY EAT ONE EGG?

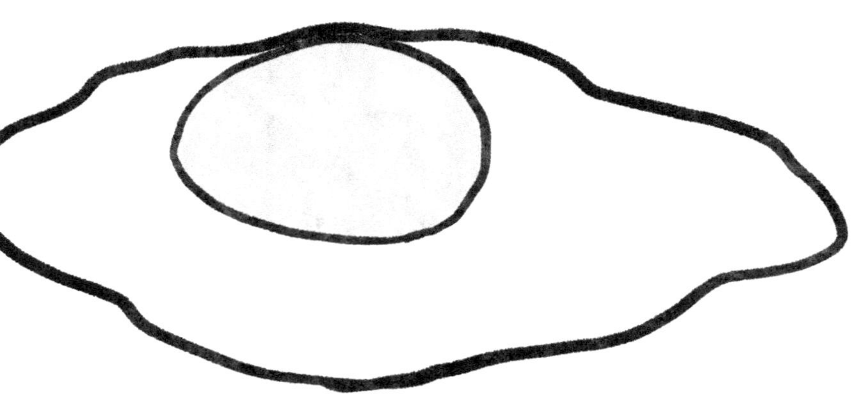

BECAUSE ONE EGG IS UN OEUF.

DO YOU KNOW WHAT I LOVE
ABOUT SWITZERLAND?

WELL, THE FLAG IS A BIG PLUS.

WHAT DO YOU CALL SOMEONE WHO USED TO WORK IN A MINE?

DOUG.

WHAT DO YOU COOK INDIAN FLATBREAD IN?

A NAAN stick PAN.

I'M HOPING MY BREAD TURNS out ok....!

FINGERS CRUST.

WHAT NAME DO YOU GIVE A SHOE MADE FROM A BANANA SKiN?

A SLiPPER.

I DON'T KNOW WHAT APOCALYPSE MEANS.

I DON'T THINK IT'S THE END OF THE WORLD.

I WAS EATING PASTA ON MY OWN.

NOW I FEEL CANNELLONI.

USED TO BE SCARED OF SPEED BUMPS.

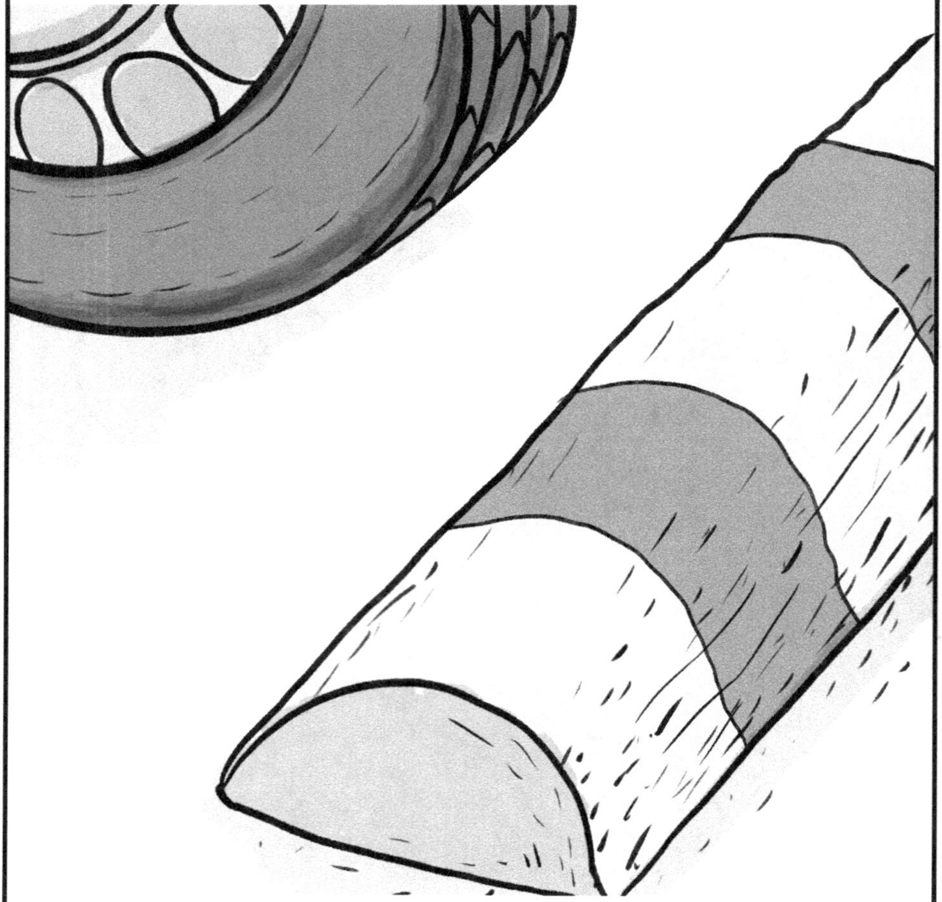

BUT I'M SLOWLY GETTING OVER IT.

WHAT FISH WORK IN HOSPITALS?

STURGEONS.

DIARRHEA IS HEREDITARY.

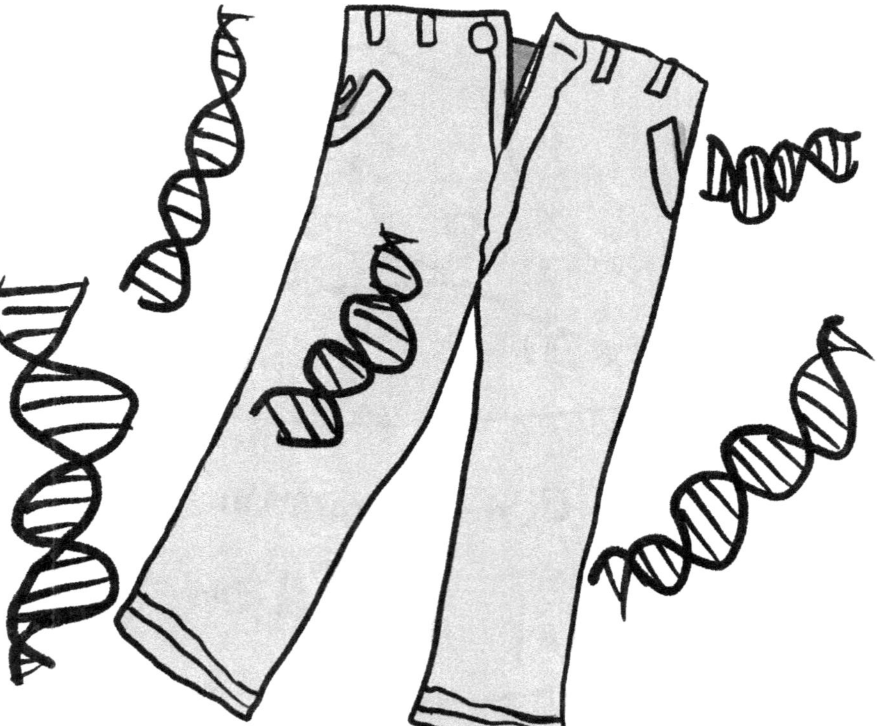

IT RUNS IN THE JEANS.

MY BROTHER AND I LAUGH ABOUT HOW COMPETITIVE WE ARE...

BUT I LAUGH MORE.

WHY DON'T VAMPIRES GAMBLE?

THEY DON'T like THE STAKES.

I DON'T tell DAD jokes.

BUt WHEN I DO, HE lAUGHS.

HOW DO YOU SPELL PANDA?

JUST TAKE P AND A.

I STOPPED WEARING GLASSES.

I'D SEEN ENOUGH.

HOW DO YOU MAKE ONE DISAPPEAR?

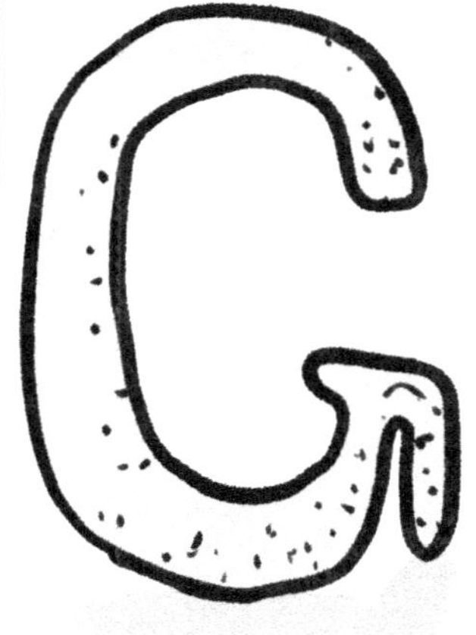 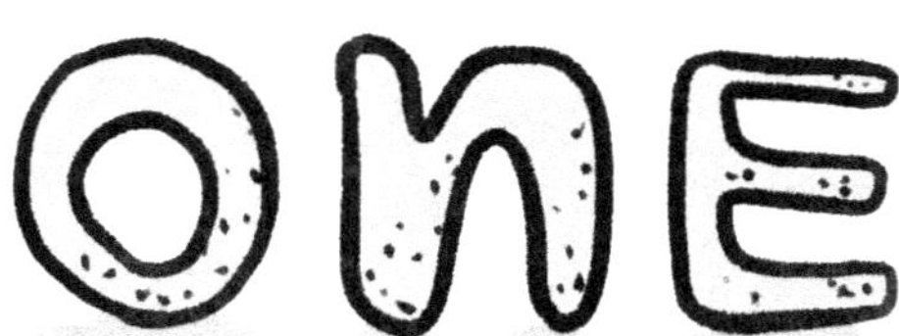

ADD A G, AND IT'S GONE.

I THINK I'D BE A GOOD WAITER.

I BRING A lot to THE TABLE.

NOW THAT HARRY HAS GIVEN UP HIS ROYAL TITLE,

HE'S THE ARTIST FORMERLY KNOWN AS PRINCE.

WHAT DID THE SEA SAY TO THE BEACH?

NOTHING, IT JUST WAVED.

I KNOW A JOKE ABOUT ROOFS.

NEVER MIND, IT WILL GO OVER YOUR HEAD.

THE FiRST FRENCH FRY WASN'T ACTUALLY MADE IN FRANCE.

It WAS FRIED IN GREECE.

WHY DID THE CRIMINAL SIT DOWN?

BECAUSE HE NEEDED ARREST.

DID YOU HEAR ABOUT THE NUT
THAT SNEEZES?

A CASH-EW.

WHAT ARE A COW'S FAVOURITE MAGAZINES?

cattlelogs.

CAN YOU MAKE CHEESE IN THE AFTERLIFE?

NO, THERE'S NOW WHEY IN HELL.

WHAT WOULD HAPPEN IF AMERICANS SWITCHED FROM POUNDS TO kILOGRAMS?

MASS CONFUSION.

I WAS GIVEN A FRIDGE AS A PRESENT.

MY FACE lit UP WHEN I OPENED it.

I SAW AN APE WEARING UNDERWEAR.

THEY WERE CHIMP PANTS, SEE?

WHY ARE PEOPLE FROM MOSCOW OUT OF BREATH?

THEY ARE ALWAYS RUSSIAN.

WHAT DO YOU CALL A SUPERHERO WHO LIKES GOING FOR WALKS?

WANDER WOMAN.

WHY WAS THE COW SAD?

IT WAS FEELING MOO-DY.

I HAVE THE PSYCHIC ABILITY to PREDICT WHAT IS IN PRESENTS.

It IS A GIFT.

AUSTRALIANS DON'T LIKE DESSERTS MADE FROM EGG WHITES AND SUGAR.

THEY BOO MERINGUE.

IF YOU BOIL A FUNNY BONE,

YOU GET A laughing stock.

WHEN IS AN IPOD like the TITANIC?

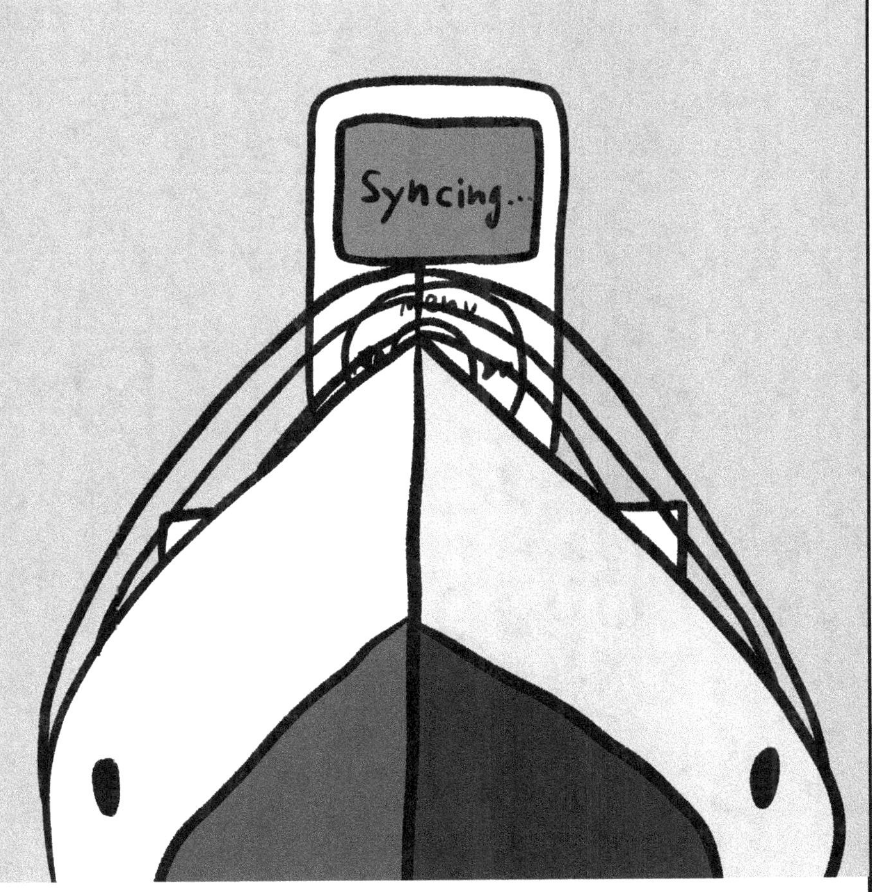

WHEN IT'S SYNCING.

I GLUED MYSELF TO MY AUTOBIOGRAPHY.

THAT'S MY STORY, AND I'M STICKING TO IT.

DOCTORS LIKE TESTING REFLEXES BY TAPPING KNEES.

THEY FIND THEY GET A KICK OUT OF IT.

I SAW SOMEONE FALL OVER CARRYING SOME IRONED CLOTHES.

I WATCHED it ALL UNFOLD.

WHY DO POLICE USE BEES?

FOR STING OPERATIONS.

DO YOU LIKE EGG JOKES?

THEY CRACK ME UP.

A WOMAN WAS CAUGHT WITH DRUGS IN HER BRA.

POLICE SAID IT WAS A BIG BUST.

SEA BIRDS BELIEVE ANYTHING.

THEY ARE SO GULL-iBLE.

WHY WAS THE DUCK BANKRUPT?

HE HAD A BIG BILL.

TIME FLIES LIKE AN ARROW.

FRUIT FLIES LIKE A BANANA.

CAN BEER MAKE YOU MORE intelligent?

YES, it MADE BUD WISER.

I JOGGED A MILE A DAY FOR A MONTH.

NOW I DON'T KNOW WHERE I AM.

IT'S EASY TO SMUGGLE CHOCOLATE INTO A CINEMA.

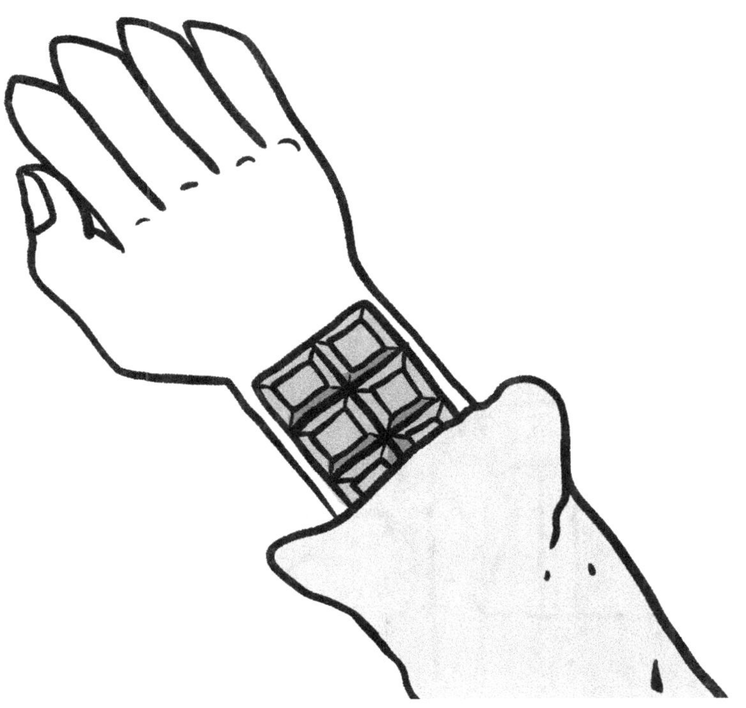

YOU JUST NEED TO HAVE A FEW TWIX UP YOUR SLEEVES.

SATURDAY AND SUNDAY ARE THE STRONGEST DAYS.

ALL THE OTHERS ARE WEEKDAYS.

I BOUGHT MY GRANDDAD A SNOWBOARD, AND HE DIED SOON AFTER.

HE WENT DOWNHILL qUICKLY.

WHAT DO YOU DO IF A TAP IS stuck?

YOU HAVE TO FAUCET.

A WAITER SAW MY UNEATEN FOOD AND SAID: "DO YOU WANT A BOX FOR THAT?"

I REPLIED "NO, BUT LET'S WRESTLE FOR IT."

IF YOU'RE AT AN AIRPORT AND YOU EVERYONE'S BAGS ARE BETTER THAN YOURS...

IT'S THE WORST-CASE SCENARIO.

WHAT DO YOU CALL A GROUP OF MEN WAITING TO HAVE THEIR HAIR CUT?

A BARBER QUEUE.

I LOST MY DVD OF GONE IN 60 SECONDS.

IT WAS HERE A MINUTE AGO.

I ACCIDENTALLY KICKED SOME ICE CUBES UNDER THE FRIDGE.

I DON'T MIND, THOUGH, it's ALL WATER UNDER THE BRIDGE.

WHAT DO YOU CALL BEES WHEN THEY CAN'T DECIDE?

A MAYBE.

WHAT JOB DID THE LAWYER DO IN THE KITCHEN?

SUE CHEF.

I WAS ADDICTED TO VIAGRA.

IT WAS PROBABLY THE HARDEST TIME I EVER HAD.

I CAN'T DECIDE IF I HAVE HEAD lice

IT'S A REAL HEAD-SCRATCHER.

HOW DO YOU KILL A CIRCUS?

GO FOR THE JUGGLER.

MY LANDLORD WANTS TO COME ROUND AND ASK ME WHY MY HEATING BILL IS SO HIGH.

I SAID MY DOOR IS ALWAYS OPEN.

THE INVENTION OF THE UNIVERSAL REMOTE CONTROL WAS MASSIVE.

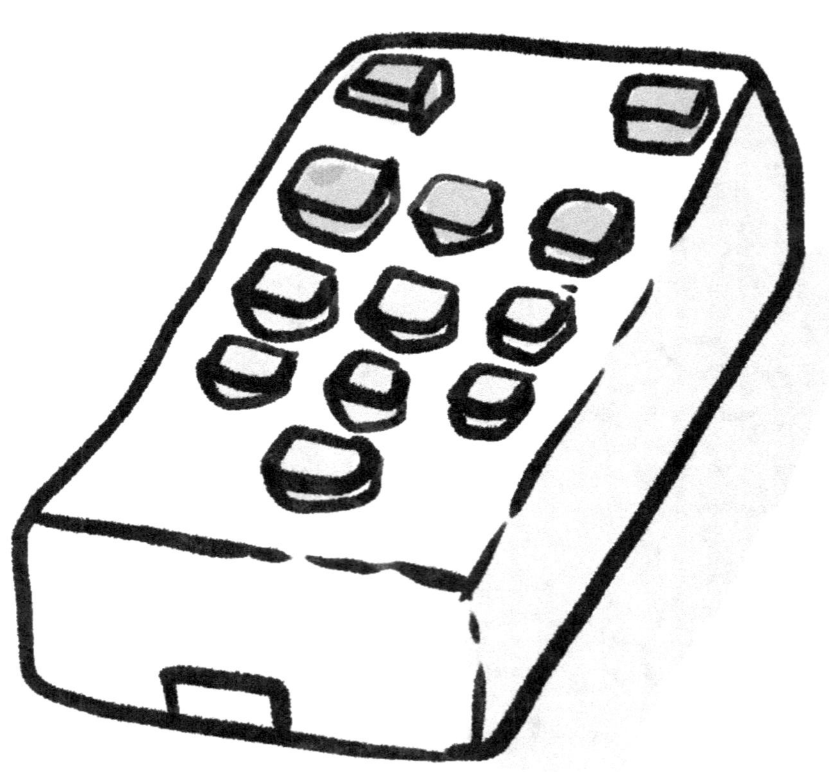

IT CHANGED EVERYTHING.

DID YOU HEAR ABOUT THE CROSS-EYED TEACHER?

HE COULDN'T CONTROL HIS PUPILS.

I WANT A JOB CLEANING MIRRORS.

IT'S SOMETHING I CAN DEFINITELY SEE MYSELF DOING.

WHAT NOISE DO GRAPES MAKE WHEN YOU STEP ON THEM?

THEY LET OUT A little WINE.

DO FRENCH PEOPLE PLAY COMPUTER GAMES?

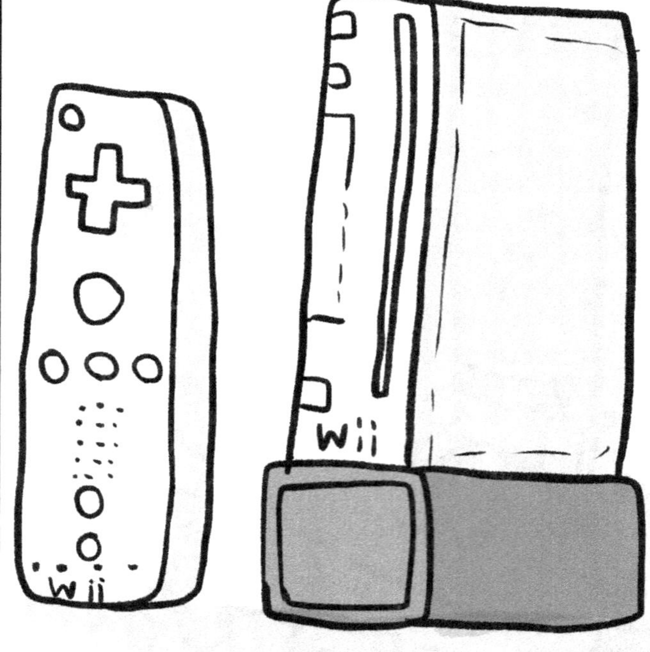

Wii.

HOW DO YOU THINK THE UNTHINKABLE?

WITH AN iTHEBERG.

WHY ARE SUPERHEROES BAD AT tests?

THEY ARE ALWAYS WRITING WRONGS.

I DON'T TRUST TREES.

THEY ARE ALL A BIT SHADY.

WHAT DO YOU CALL THE MOST POPULAR BASEMENT?

THE BEST CELLAR.

WHAT DO YOU CALL A FUNNY lizARD?

A STAND UP CHAMELEON.